SURF ADVENTURES OF NOAH

story and pictures by blake hill

To my beautiful Leo, Pumpkin Pie and Tiger...
I love you guys!

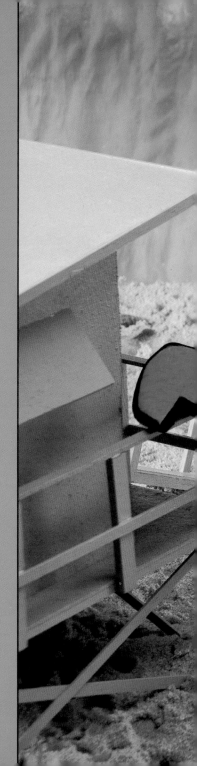

Noah and Dad race over the sand.
Their boards tucked tightly
in their hands.

"The waves are reelin',"
Dad says with a smile,
"Be careful—or you and your board
will end up in a pile."

They give thanks for this beautiful day,
And ask **Mother Ocean** permission to play.

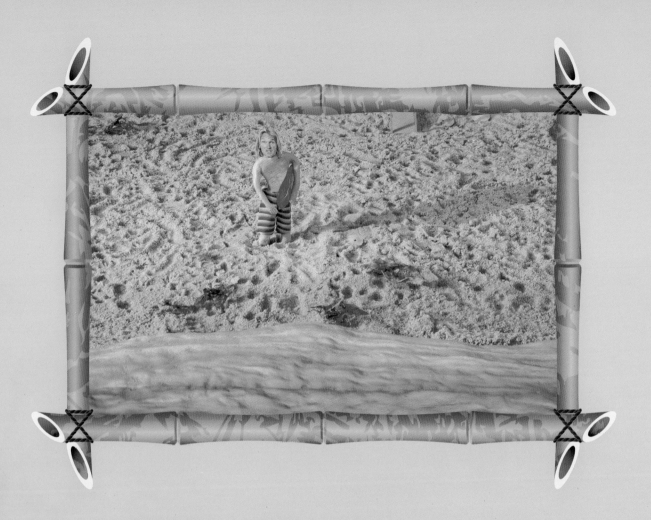
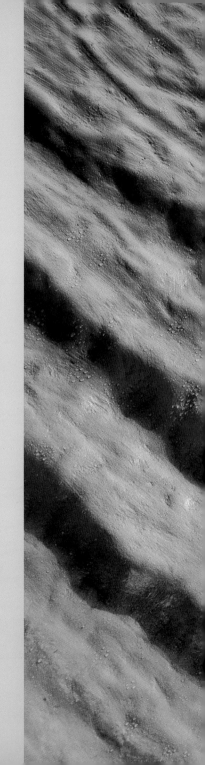

Big Dad turns to Noah and asks
"Where are you paddling out?"
But to Big Dad's dismay Noah's already out
without giving a scout.

Dad watches as Noah struggles with grace
to find his surfing place.
Big Dad's intuition alerts him to stand tall
in the sand, just in case.

A mom and baby Dolphin stretch out in the surf.
As a friendly Seal barks out a morning tune
in his beach break turf.

Now Noah's stuck in a dangerous place
as the waves grow bigger in size.
He understands that his haste to paddle
has left him feeling unwise.

Noah turns to catch the next big wave
but his position is too far inside.
When he leaps to his feet, the inevitable happens
and he loses his sweet surfing glide.

WIPEOUT!

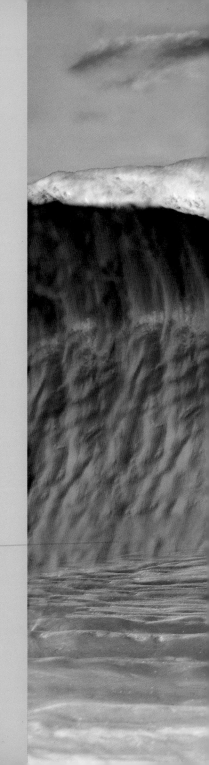

The Seal and Dolphins watch from afar
as Noah tumbles over the falls.
Big Dad catches his breath
as Noah pops up in the white wash crawl.

Big Dad stands with his toes dug in the sand.
He's thrilled to see Noah walking on land.

He puts his arm around his son
as they sit on the beach discussing the spin.
Noah stares at the sand and says with a whisper,
"I'm not sure if I'm going back in."

As Noah talks, Big Dad listens.
The waves calm down and the water glistens.

"I went out too soon before watching the break.
The waves seemed small for anyone to take."

Big Dad says, "That's a great observation.
What is your plan?"
Noah says, "I'll sit here on land
with my feet in the sand."

They both laugh while enJoying the sun.
The Sea Gull squaks, "Go have some fun."

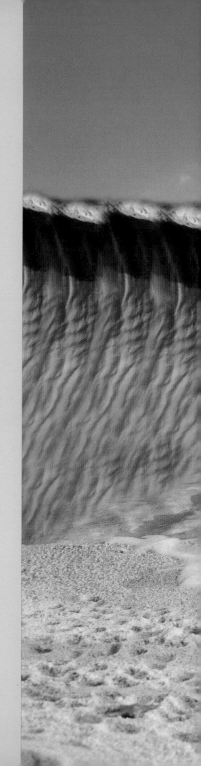

Noah is scared of his place in the ocean
and feels unsure as he checks the waves' motion.

At last Noah turns to his dad and asks,
"Do you think I'm ready to surf again?"
Big Dad smiles with loving support,
"You could ask your wisdom within."

Noah's courage rises to the top.
His instincts and inner voice have told him
go hop.

Noah rips a cutback across the face of the wave.
His board shoots a spray so brave.
Dad stands tall with his arms out wide.
"I'm proud of you Noah, now rip a tail slide!"

Big or Small
Short or Tall
Have a Ball
Even when you Fall!

Live, Love, Surf. ALOHA!

Surf Adventures of Noah
Wipeout
Book One
Text and photographs © 2010 by Blake Hill

All photographs*: Blake Hill
*Except Page 47, courtesy Mike Riggins © 2010
Lighting: Jay Yowler
Lighting assistant: Brogan Dunphy
Book and cover design: Brad Miskell

ISBN 978-0-9827351-0-7

Library of Congress Control Number: 2010905483

Lil' Ripper Clothing ®, LiL-Ripper.com
www.bolt-boards.com

BOLT PUBLISHING
6100 Center Dr Suite 600
Los Angeles, CA 90045
www.bolt-publishing.com

Printed in China